S T O P

DATING UNTIL .....

BY

RITA RICHARDSON JACKSON

STOP DATING UNTIL ......

DEDICATION

This book is dedicated to my two daughters Natalie Brooke Jackson, and Brandice Victoria Jackson

Book Description

Stop Dating Until ... is a commitment blueprint for every woman that has ever been dumped, played, let-go of after giving the relationship her all, ghosted on, had up to 3 relationships to go up in flames in a year, or for women that stayed "on point" in a long term relationship until it was apparent that a proposal for marriage was not forth-coming, even after 5, 6, 7 8, 9, 10 years or more!

It's not necessarily that you are doing anything (or everything) wrong, either! In fact, as a Life Coach and relationship strategist, with over 25 years of experience, I have found a common variable that exist for highly successful women is that they tend to be "over-functioning" and doing too much too soon. They may even take charge of the relationship, and become the aggressor, throughout the courting and dating phase of their relationship(s). The same assertive work ethic in the business and corporate world may back-fire on the women over achievers, in a dating relationship! Doing the absolute most, too soon, throughout the relationship, will weaken or completely take away a man's opportunity to naturally develop commitment, that can lead to a proposal and marriage!

Never again will you have to wonder (or ask a guy that you are dating) if you are his girlfriend, or be lead into a relationship trap of locking yourself down! That's his job! Ladies, if you're ready to attract men of integrity, weed out players, and non-committal time wasters, "Stop Dating Until ..." you read this book, by Rita Richardson Jackson! It is an award-winning guide to purposeful dating that leads to commitment to women by men.

ACKNOWLEDGMENTS

Thank you to members of my groups: Sip & See Singles, Marry Me Singles, Singles Interested. In Getting Married, and Marriage On Demand

TABLE OF CONTENT

INTRODUCTION

This book will dramatically empower your life as a woman, by changing the way you look at men and dating. It will also teach you valuable secrets that will uncover your natural abilities to control your relationships and have men at your feet. Once you are able to alter your perception and use Rita Jackson's Stop Dating Until book, you will be able to incorporate your secret feminine powers, into your own brand. This will empower you and support your overall success in other areas of your life, also!

If you've had a string of bad relationships, **you will learn how to effortlessly break this cycle and gain an understanding of how to "weed out" time wasters, stringers, and players!**

Every woman has the potential to attract the man of her dreams, make him fall head over heels in love with her, and give her everything she has ever wanted, including marriage.

It doesn't matter if you are fat, short, tall, skinny, or shy. You could be a woman who's 19 and single, or 43 and divorced for the third time. Whoever you are and whatever you're going through, you carry the potential within you to completely change your outcomes with men. I am sure you have seen an array of examples of women who manage the impossible.

The attractive woman with the good-looking man that makes you think "what does he see in her?" And there's the woman you know that is a complete "B" and yet her man is at her beck and call! To top it off, there are the women who have men at their disposal buying them gifts and never hesitating to treat them like princesses.

Have you ever wondered why some women can get men to treat them well, while other women struggle with their relationships? What are these women doing that the other women aren't? I can tell you that these women don't fall into these situations accidently!

While it is true that some women are able to do this naturally, there are many women that utilize strategy, relationship rules that incorporate **Relationship Markers** (that will be defined and discussed later on in a separate chapter). The latter group of women, intentionally influence the male mind by using their charm and practices that all women possess (and can utilize).

A woman's success plan must incorporate her **brand,** and utilize relationship practices that will help her to identify her powers, over men, and how to use those powers in the most effective ways, to achieve her relationship goal of getting married one day.

The information in this book will teach you how to effectively use (and work) your personal action plan, to get yourself and your "Mr. Right" to the wedding altar in as little as one year, or less.

Unfortunately many women will go through life without this knowledge. Instead they will instinctively go with the flow of love following destiny, and only end up hurt in the end.

Some of us women fall for a person so hard we end up being hurt by them repeatedly! And yet, there are some of us that get hurt by a man and learn from the mistakes, only to move on to another man who is hurting us in a completely different way! The best thing to do is to let this make us better, not bitter, and "Stop Dating Until" we figure out what's going on!

Not all men are cold hearted! There are some really awesome men out there! I know because I married one!

Here's my story:

Within six months, my guy proposed on bended knee, and we were married within the year. Although, I didn't have a book like this, as a reference, my mother and ladies in my family, passed on a few relationship guidelines that I will share with you. However, I suggest that before you continuing reading this book, I must ask for three things (from you): **Courage, Commitment, and Change.** Your commitment to follow through and your courage to change will directly reflect your success.

Whatever you've been doing (or not doing) hasn't worked! And if you continue to do what you have always done, you will continue to get more of the same results!

So, I want you to repeat after me: "It's time for me to make a few changes! I want to start experiencing a different outcome with men."

No doubt, you already have a certain mindset and attitude about men and dating. Consequently, this old belief system (that has not served you well) will have to be replaced with a brand-new belief system!

Growth, can be uncomfortable, and may seem impossible at first! However, with a little bit of discipline and determination, you will be able to change your outcome with men! Trust and believe, you'll get the hang of it, and it will become second nature to you! Soon, your successes will far outnumber your failures.

What to Expect During Transition

At times you may find it awkward to put the advice into action. Just realize that this uncomfortable feeling is part of changing.

Visualization is the process of creating pictures in your mind of yourself enjoying what you want. When you visualize, you generate powerful thoughts and feelings of having it now. The law of attraction then returns that reality to you, just as you saw it in your mind

Be brave enough to embrace the discomfort and move forward. With practices and time, it will begin to feel normal. Just like learning to ride a bike, at first it seemed impossible! However, after a few practice runs you get the hang of it and now you can ride a bike with ease. Learning a new style of interacting with men and will be the same way! Once you're able to let go of previous ways of thinking about men and dating, a completely new world awaits you. You'll have men lining up to date you, desperate for your attention, and eager to please you! You'll never be sad over men again you won't be cheated on lied to or let down by men ever again.

Your "Mr. Right" will find you through attraction! In fact, he may be someone that you already have a friendship with! Check out the men that already like you, and are always there for you! Trust me, you can easily make him fall madly in love with you, and never want to leave you. Best of all you'll be having the time of your life while doing it!

Since the beginning of time, men have had us (women) figured out. They know how to manipulate us, lie to us, cheat on us, play with our minds, and tear out our hearts! Even worse, is their ability to keep us around, even after they have done all of those terrible things! The question that begs an answer is: How did they get so good at it? And the answer is: They know our weakness, and that is -- our emotions!

Every human being has emotions. In order for you to be able to control your emotions, you will, now, take the time to think of how you are going to reign in yours.

1. Make a list of emotions
2. Next, revisit how you usually handle your emotions.

3. What will you need to do to keep your emotions in check and under your control?

Knowledge is Power:

The Schematic Diagram (of The Commitment Blueprint) Explained

Courting --- (Dates 1, 2, 3, 4, up to – 8 weeks)➔ The courting phase starts at point zero on the schematic diagram of the relationship continuum. **The courting phase continues until the guy that you are friendly dating, formally asks you to be his "Girlfriend," and you say yes.**

Please note: A man asking a woman to be his girlfriend is the first step or action (taken by him) that will guide him along the pathway of developing a commitment (to you).

Yes, this simple request from him, asking you to be his girlfriend, initiates the process and the order of how things will operate (on this commitment model).

The man is expected to do the asking, thereby demonstrating that he is ready to take on the responsibilities, also, that comes with you accepting his proposal to be his girlfriend!

A woman should never have to wonder what she means to a guy or what her "formal" title is.

During the Courting Phase, you are simply his friend, and you will remain casual dating friends, until your friend asks you to be his girlfriend!

Until a man asks a woman to be his girlfriend, the woman must treat him as the social acquaintance/friend that he is! No matter how handsome and charming, you find him to be, you must control your emotions, and avoid over performing your status: Acquaintance/friend. When a man is motivated to be more than a casual friend to a woman, he will do amazing things to win her over, including asking her to be his girlfriend. When a man is really "into" a woman, he respects boundaries

In purposeful dating, it is important for a woman to "fall back" and let a man take the lead in demonstrating that he is serious about moving your friendship into a relationship, through purposeful dating. Next, you will be guided through my purposeful dating Commitment Blueprint: "Before You Start!"

BEFORE YOU START

DECIDE and SET YOUR BOUNDARIES

BRAND/STYLE

MARKETING TO ATTRACT YOUR GUY

PURPOSEFUL ACTIVITIES

SELF DATING FOR ENTERTAINMENT

RELAX! HAVE FUN but NO SEX/HEAVY KISSING/TOUCHING
FOR THE FIRST 90 DAYS/3 MONTHS

RULES

STRATEGIC ACTIONS

1. DATING PHASE

DATE # 1

DATE # 2

DATE # 3

MAN ASK WOMAN TO BE HIS
OFFICIAL GIRLFRIEND

5 QUESTIONS TO ASK HIM

5 COMMITMENT QUESTIONS

2. DATING PHASE

DATE # 4

DATE # 5

DATE # 6

DATE # 7

DATE # 8

PRINCE CHARMING / RIDE OR DIE TEST

60 DAY / 2 MONTHS RULE GUIDELINES

DATE # 9

DATE # 10

DATE # 11

DATE # 12

DATE # 13

DATE # 14

DATE # 15

DATE # 16

90 DAY RULE GUIDELINES

DECIDE TO KEEP DATING OR
RETURN TO THE COURTING PHASE

A PROPOSAL OF MARRIAGE
BETWEEN DATE 12 - 32

Marriage On Demand
ATIR Publishing

At the end of date 32 /6 months

A COMMITMENT TO MARRIAGE OR RETURN TO COURT NEW GUY

Twenty-five Reasons to Stop Dating Until ...

By Rita Richardson Jackson

Stop Dating Until ...

1. You are ready to **be serious about committing**. "If you don't mind being a serial dater and you're not serious about committing, then, by all means, do as you please, but make sure the other person is on the same page and that you're aware it may not last. Understand this: having a good relationship depends on the structure of the foundation on which it is built! If you fail to plan for the success of your new relationship, then you plan to fail. Plan to pay attention to acknowledged relationship indicators that lead to commitment, loyalty, and respect!

Stop Dating Until ...

2. You are ready to **let go of past baggage and insecurities**. Insecurity breeds jealousy, and too much of that is a relationship killer.

Dating can be scary. It's basically like an audition or interview. If you're constantly feeling like you're not attractive enough, smart enough, or worthy enough in any type of way, things may get rough for you until you figure out how to get over these feelings.

Stop Dating Until ...

3. You **know who you are, and have defined yourself**. Otherwise, you'll end up pretending to be who you don't intend to be! You can be fake for only so long, before the real you emerges! If you are not the happy home-maker type of woman that enjoys cooking, cleaning, and catering to her man, then don't pretend to be that sort of woman. Having your suit fall in love with a mirage, and turning into the "real" you later on the relationship will end badly! Perhaps you are a career-minded woman that hates everything about homemaking, and would rather have a cook and maids! Or, you may be bossy and a little controlling? No problem, stay patient, until you attract a suitor that is looking to be directed (by you)! There are tons of suitors out there, so never settle! Be your authentic self!

Stop Dating Until ...

4. You **know what your emotional needs are, and how to control them**. Don't be so busy ticking things off your mental list as the other person speaks, that you're not even paying attention to them when they attempt to **express who they really are."** Stay woke, and not too impressed by flattery!

Stop Dating Until ...

5. You can **be a good listener**. The foundation of a good relationship includes the ability to listen. Not just hearing what someone says to you and taking from it what you want, but the actual work of listening to what someone says without turning it into something about yourself

Stop Dating Until ....

6. You can **resist the urge to paint a different picture, of who your suitor is, after they have shown you their true colors**. If a suitor loses his temper easily with you or others, believe this: he has an anger management problem that needs to be addressed. If a suitor disrespects other women, but not you, yet, sooner or later he will get around to

disrespecting you, too, if you stay in the relationship long enough.

Stop Dating Until ....

7. You **have a clear understanding of your purpose for dating**. The idea of dating (after the courtship) is to **screen for a new partner**, hopefully, a long lasting one. If you're in the market for someone to call, text, and be with you, then you'll have to make room.

    As much as you want your partner to bring all good things to the table, they are wanting the same thing from you. Think about what you bring to a relationship, both positive attributes, and flawed ones. Are you reliable? Are you honest? Are you a good listener? Do you have a bad temper? Are you insecure? Are you jealous? Are you affectionate? Do you want children? Do you already have children? And you can add additional things to this list.

Stop Dating Until ....

8. You can **fall back, stay in your own line, and not take over**. Don't assume the role of the aggressor in the relationship. Allow yourself to be perused (or not). Because men are natural aggressors, you need to fall back, and allow

a man to be "the man!" When a man is interested in a woman, there is no mountain too high for him to climb over to get to her! Allow him to do what he does best. Never hunt down a man or chase after him!

Stop Dating Until ....

9. You can **project yourself in such a way that discourages time-wasting "players!"** Develop your brand in the way you speak, walk, and dress. Just by the way you carry yourself will give an impression. Remember, you will never get a second chance to make a first impression.

Stop Dating Until ....

10. You can be abstinent during the friendship/courting phase as you are getting to know each other. Remember, there should be not forms of intimacy during the courting – get-to - know you phase (of developing a **relationship of commitment**)! The thought of allowing one strange suitor after the next, have intimate (kissy, touchy, feely) contact with you, makes no sense on so many levels! There will plenty of time for appropriate displays of affection, once he has asked you to be his girlfriend and you have said yes! Until

then, treat him like the acquaintance that he is: A man trying to prove that he is worthy of you!

Stop Dating Until ….

11. You can hold yourself back **(during the courtship)** from acting like your suitor's "girlfriend," until you've been formally **asked by your suitor to be their girlfriend**, and you choose to accept. **You** are nobody's girlfriend until they have asked you to be, and you have accepted the title. **DO not skip this step!** In fact, this is your suitor's first proposal (to you): "Will you be my girlfriend!" Until then, you are simply two strangers getting to know more about each other, so that you can make an informed decision about moving on to dating each other.

Stop Dating Until ….

12. You have established (in your mind) what the appropriate, respectful behavior will be between yourself and any new suitor that you barely know. It would be wise to refrain form any form of intimacy, during this courting (get to know you) phase. Additionally, you should not engage in PDA (public displays of affection) until you have officially been asked by your suitor, to be his girlfriend.

Stop Dating Until ....

13. You **understand (and embrace) this concept: How others treat you is determined by what you tolerate, and are willing to accept.** One thing is certain: You have got to stop playing the blame game, and pointing your finger at someone else about their treatment of you! Suitors and other people in general, will walk all over you, if you allow them to do so! You must admit that 50% of what has happened to you and will continue to happen to you is your own fault. Remember this: "It takes two to tango!" – You and the other person!

Stop Dating Until ....

14. You can accept and be ready to stand your ground on this relationship concept: **It is not your job or responsibility to lock yourself down, at any point during the relationship. That's your suitor's job/responsibility.** Make up your mind that until a man has locked you down (and put a ring on it) refuse to lock yourself down, or function as his "wifee!" That's on you, if you do!

    Being (and functioning as) a free spirited woman with no constraints or boundaries, may feel good for both the woman and her suitor, at first. However, this type of relationship without boundaries may not work out too well for a woman. Case in point is the woman that finds herself in a going nowhere relationship for 5 to 10 years (or more) with a man that has shown no plans to lock her down as his wife!

However, the woman chooses to stay, because of the time and effort that she has put into the relationship trying to prove that she is good enough and deserving to be his wife! He may, now, treat her as if he doesn't care if she goes or stay (in his life). He may even justify his dis-loyalty and cheating on her by reminding her that he never asked her to be his girlfriend, anyway!

Ladies, if you have to ask a man if you are his girlfriend, and he has never asked you to be his girlfriend, then you need to stop dating him, fall all the way back, and stop dating him, unless you enjoy your role (and title of) "friend with sexual benefits" (for him) and/or his unofficial "wifee!" at best!

Stop Dating Until …

15. You have a predetermined end point for your dating phase (of not more than 6 months). By this time, you should both

know where this relationship is headed: To the wedding altar, or nowhere?

You can walk away from an undefined dating relationship after a reasonable amount of your time, usually, about 6 months. My research has turned up that men that are of the "marrying kind" propose with a ring on bended knee, within 3 – 6 months, and marries her during the following 6 to 12 months. Fact: You are enough, just as you are! If a suitor has shown no intention to marry you, by the end of the first 6 months of dating, it's time to give him the boot, stop the dating (with him) and allow yourself to be courted by a new suitor(s)! Now, you can see the value in NOT having sex with any suitor, too soon. At the end of the 6 month dating phase, it's okay to shake hands, and say goodbye!

Stop Dating Until ….

16. You can have strategic and meaningful discussions with your suitor that includes your suitor's interest in marriage in general, and having kids, specifically. During the "get to know you" courting phase, it is important to skillfully interview your suitor, and to be honest about who you are and what you want out of a relationship! If you are looking for a suitor that is interested in getting married and having

children, sometime during the courtship, these topics should be tactfully brought up and discussed.

Stop Dating Until ....

17. You have tested your suitor's loyalty, dependability, and their loyalty (to you. Are you his only girlfriend? Does this suitor understand what your **emotional** needs are and does he satisfy them? Do you know what your suitor's emotional needs are, and are you willing to satisfy them? The bottom line is this: There is a lot **to get to know** about another person, so do not rush in to an imaginary world of walking down the wedding aisle, and having his babies!

Stop Dating Until ....

18. You can **stop yourself** from acting like a thirsty, impressionable, gold-digger. For some suitors, giving gifts and offering weekend trips is a part of what they do to each woman that they meet! It doesn't mean that they love, respect, intend to marry, respect, or will be loyal to you! Therefore, you must be prepared to turn down certain gifts, such as a romantic weekend trip. A romantic travel proposal that is accepted too early, during the dating phase can put a woman in a very awkward position of being inappropriately

intimate, too soon. There will be plenty of time for all of these things, after he has demonstrated his integrity, loyalty, honesty, and commitment to you, after you are engaged or (better still) after you are his wife! Don't act so impressed over going on an out of town trip, or a designer purse. These are just material things! Until he pops the question "will you marry me?" don't be impressed!

Stop Dating Until ....

19. You know what your goal is for dating, and are willing to practice purposeful dating with that specific goal, ever present, in your mind and actions! Really, it's as simple as this: Less is always more for your suitor to try harder to show you that he is worth it! When a man loves a woman, he will do the over performing. However, you have to fall all the way back to give him the space, time, and opportunity. Never throw yourself at a suitor!

Stop Dating Until ....

20. You can pace your actions without over-reaching or performing! Until you are his girlfriend, don't do any of the things a girlfriend does. Until you are legally married, don't do anything that a wife does. At each phase of your

relationship, stay in your lane. You will save yourself a lot of heartache and disappointment.

Stop Dating Until ....

21. You can be alone, date yourself, and accept responsibility for your own happiness. Happiness is an inside job! It is not healthy for anybody to rely upon someone else to tell them who they are, such as if they are pretty, too fat, doesn't dress appropriately, or if they would be acceptable to their friends. Do not allow a suitor (or anyone) make you feel that something is wrong with you, or that if you were only a little more to their liking they'd propose and marry you! Now hear this: You mare enough. You are good enough just as you are!

Stop Dating Until ....

22. You have completed your self-branding (inside and out), in a way that will convey to all that sees you, "this is who I am," and I am awesome! Whether or not you agree with it, men are attracted with what they first see: the way you look in your clothes, and your expressive personality! Whatever you want others to think of you has to be on point, every time you walk outside! Remember this: You never get a second chance to make a first impression!

Stop Dating Until ....

23. You have figured out what went wrong in your previous relationships to some degree - or get to the point where you've learned *something. Until you understand your own failed relationship(s), you are doomed to repeat the same mistakes!* Consider this: If you have been dumped or cheated on by each of the men that you have dated, it is time for you to stop dating until you can face the real reason(s) behind this!

Stop Dating Until ....

24. You can figure out why your suitors "ghost-out" on you! This especially true, if you've put time and effort into a person, gone out with them several times, had "sleepovers," changed your relationship status on social media, they've met your family - *and you've done this at least 2 times in the last year*!!!! Consider this: - a dating "time-out" may be in order.

Stop Dating Until ....

25. You are empowered and able to say to the world: **I am enough just as I am**. Now, what lucky man wants to earn my attention, my loyalty, my love, marry me, and have children with me?

Knowing your own strengths and weaknesses will underscore, in positive ways, your self-esteem. When you accept and respect yourself with imperfections and all, others that you interact with can do no less! You are enough, just as you are!

Stop Dating until ...

You have an understanding of Relationship Markers

Whether you already have a guy, looking to find one to marry, you're on your first marriage or your fourth! Understanding what Relationship Markers are will help you to discover:

* If your guy is the marrying kind, or not

* Will he commit to marriage (with you) or not.

* What will motivate a man to take you to the altar

* Whether you (and your guy) have nothing more than "friends with benefits" relationship.

Relationship Markers will help you to make a realistic assessment of your relationship and offer a fresh perspective on how your man's mind works.

A Relationship Marker is based on truth telling, self-positioning, and branding. In the right proportions, this combination yields dynamic marketing tactics to reel in your king!

In my line of work as an online Life Coach, specializing in dating, relationships and sexuality concerns, I have a keen sense of male /female interaction. After being in the business for over 25 years, I know exactly what it takes to get even the biggest commitment-phoebes to his most uncomfortable position: down on bended knee!

No, you don't have to be the prettiest, richest, or thinnest woman to get him to commit, and to close the deal! There's an art and sexy charm to it! Having grown up in Alabama in a large family of church going women, understanding men (and how to please them), was a perpetual topic of discussion, in our pastime! In fact, there were discussions on the tasteful art of flirting, speaking, and carrying oneself in the presence of men, in general. True queens, know how the art of attracting Kingly men to her without uttering one word! Men, in general, love everything about women! The way we smell, the way we feel, the movement of our hips, our voice, how we look, and yes, our "hotness!" It takes less than 30 seconds or less for a man to decide if he wants to approach you (or not).

RELATIONSHIP MARKERS DEFINED

By Rita Richardson Jackson

A **Relationship Marker** is a green light indicator that a couple may earn for taking specific positive actions, from the courtship period to closing the deal with a proposal and marriage.

Relationship Marker # 1 (Courting)

The first relationship marker is awarded to a couple**, <u>at the end of the courtship period</u>**, when a guy asks you to be his girlfriend, and you choose to accept the title.

By the time a woman chooses to accept a man's proposal to be his girlfriend, she should have a pretty good idea about his level of respect for her boundaries, and his loyalty to her during this dating phase.

Relationship Marker # 2 (Dating)

The second relationship Marker is awarded to a couple when:

1. The man passes the woman's "Knight in Shining Amour" test of dependability

2. The man has shown himself to be a person of integrity /trust.

Obviously, each person is unique. Therefore, the time that it will take a woman to find out if her suitor is a man of integrity will vary.

Nevertheless, it is important to have a definite expiration date to allow a suitor to take up your precious time.

Therefore, a woman must be prepared to shake hands and say goodbye, if she and her suitor do not see a future together (with each other) that includes marriage, after the courting and dating phase.

A woman's success of managing (and controlling) her emotions will directly affect the success or failure of nudging her man along the relationship continuum towards the ultimate commitment of marriage.

The reason is simple: Women that believe in marriage as their ultimate "lock-down" relationship requirement, insist on it from the start, by what they say, their boundaries, and of course what they will or will not do!

Listen, ladies, if your ultimate goal is to marry a man, you must stay focused on that goal, and not get side tracked. It is all too easy for a woman to become distracted by offers of material things that may obligate you (to him) in his mind and/or yours, too. For example it would be ill advised for you to go (with him) on a romantic weekend or a week-long trip during the "courting" level of the commitment continuum. You know this and so does he. Therefore, if you can turn an opportunity like this down, politely, he will respect you for respecting yourself, and begin to fall in love with you, and see you as a woman that is not just out for his money.

Wait, slow down! Don't act so thirsty and impressed! Romantic trips, expensive gifts, having his babies and more, can be all yours, after you are his wife! Remember that! Take it from me, and other women that know the secret of how to get your man to commit!

Up to this point, you may have had a string of bad relationship experiences, but it can and will turn around for you, when you clearly demonstrate through your own behavior that you know what you want!

Men are experts at saying just the right things to women! But what are their actions demonstrating?

Stay woke! His actions will tell you all that you need to believe about his commitment to you!

Relationship Marker # 3

Training a man to respect you starts with you respecting yourself! When a man sees that you have standards, and demonstrable boundaries, they will treat you as a "high value" woman that is well worth his respect!

If you won't fall victim to his advances, too easily, he knows that he can trust that you won't do it with other men either. This builds his trust and desire for a woman of this caliber to become his wife!

Question: Do you know the difference between a girlfriend, fiancé, and a wife? In your mind and your actions, what are your boundaries for each title that you progress to, along the path to the wedding altar, and why?

Once you have this discussion with yourself and decide what your appropriate behavior will be, it will be easier for you to articulate your rationale to your suitor (present and future).

Just because a man takes you out to dinner, buys you a gift, or says nice things to you is not a reason to be intimate with him! Besides, family members and coworkers do this for you quite often with no expectations.

If you are too easy and you do everything the man (that you want to marry) ask of you from day one, you are exercising very poor judgement (and strategy).

You must be patient, stay in your lane, as a woman being pursued, and let a man "do what he does best: be the aggressor! Allow him the time to do the things that it will take to truly commit to you and earn the relationship lock-down that he desires (with you).

While he may be "drop – dead" handsome, rich, and the chemistry is there, you must adhere to this little Commitment Blueprint: No sex before engagement (if at all before marriage)

Courting phase. --- → Girlfriend -→ Dating --→ Commitment - → (Popping the Question) → Engagement -→Pre-Marriage Counseling -→Marriage

Understanding Relationship Markers will not help you to outsmart your man or trick him into walking down the aisle to the altar with you; --- it's about learning to understand him, and effortlessly **satisfying his emotional needs** to a point that makes you irreplaceable to him.

With a smile on your face, a good attitude and outlook on life, a little sway and dip in your hips, it becomes easier for him to internalize and embrace marriage (to you).

Relationship Markers highlight specific milestones along the pathway to a man's loyalty and commitment for you! Relationship markers function like a traffic light, in purposeful dating, and will separate out the "keepers" from the "creepers!".

Paying attention to relationship markers is particularly useful during the courting phase, and can help a woman to weed out would be "players" or "stringers!"

Players or stringers are men that lead the beautiful in heart, emotionally reciprocal woman along, like a puppet on a string. These men are the ultimate smooth talking time wasters that dole out smooth words and false promises of marriage and a future together.

Keep in mind that the ULTIMATE lock-down (for a woman) comes when a man proposes and marries her and NOT before! Therefore, a woman should never voluntarily put herself in relationship lock-down, or jump to "act" or function as a wife, until she is a wife.

Ladies, be patient, control your emotions, and stay in your own lane! And by all means, allow a man to be the man, and pursue you. Ladies, if you want a man to get on bended knee and ask you to marry him, allow him to do all the proving and chasing.

You Learn How to Keep a Secret

DO NOT TELL ANYONE YOUR 60 DAY, 90 Day, or 6 Month RULE!

If you tell a guy you have a 60-day, 90 Day, or 6 Month rule, he's going to stick it out just for the sex.

If you tell your friends, there's a chance they might tell on you!

This 60-day / 90-day /6-month rule is your secret.

These types of rules have been around for a long time.

Many women practice a 90-day rule or some other personal time line. Some women wait six months or more!

May sound like a long time to wait, but it's not!

We live in a fast-paced society where people meet and have sex in the same day. Well, that's them and not you.

You're a lady, and you wait at least two months (or more) for a man to prove to you he's worthy of having sex with you. The longer you make him wait, the quicker he'll will get you to the wedding altar, based upon my personal, professional experience, and the women that actually married or at least got a marriage proposal and a ring in less than 90 days (myself included) with no sexual involvement!

If you feel you can't wait that long, for whatever reason, then at the very least perform the Knight in Shining Armor "Ride or Die" Test. Understandably, you have needs, too. If your needs are that intense and you just have to have sex, then you do have other options.

I'm going to give you two options, so you have **no excuse** to break your own rule, quicker than 60 to 90 days.

Sometimes, women need (or simply want) to have sex. I understand, and I have chatted with quite a few as a sexuality consultant online.

Nevertheless, there is a time, a place, and a way to solve this little concern. Go buy a vibrator, especially, if you don't have one! Too embarrassed to go buy one? Order one discreetly online.

You Follow the rule Of No Dating Before Courting!

Courting

Courting is right on the "start-line" (at point zero) of the **Marriage On Demand Commitment Blue Print!** In fact, it is during the courting phase that a woman must control her emotions, and put into effect the **Marriage On Demand (MOD) Purposeful Dating Plan.** This is a no-nonsense approach to dating that helps a woman quickly weed out potential time wasters and stringers, before she gets too emotionally invested in them.

Dates, 1, 2, and 3 of the MOD-PDP, naturally, incorporates strategic questions that a woman can ask a new suitor, anytime that incudes but is not limited to meeting a man for the first time, or the man that you've been with for a while.

Pay attention to his answers to your questions, as well as his mannerisms (self-expression) too. Together, these two things will often reveal things about his integrity and honesty that may help a woman to decide if she leave him at relationship "start-line!" Not every man is marriage-minded or even ready to be in a relationship, and this is perfectly understandable. These are the guys that you must leave them where you found them, at "ground zero" on the relationship start-line, and keep it moving! No matter how handsome (or hot) he is, you must control your emotions, and keep it moving! No matter how pretty he tells you that you are, sweetly acknowledge his feelings, but you must keep yourself positioned and free of time wasters and players, that are experienced at telling women just the right things (1, 2 3) to emotionally entrap them. You have the power within you to break the cycle of being the emotional victim, of yet another smooth talker.

Remember this: There are two (2) individuals in a relationship! YOU must take 50% of the responsibility (good or bad) of how your relationship turns out!

My best advice to you is to be patient and slow it way down. Take your time to make each date a purposeful one. Incorporate applicable relationship questions that will help you to answer these questions:

1. Is this man relationship minded, or is he just looking for a "THOT" (That Ho Over There)?
2. Right now, who / what am I to him?
3. What do I really know about him?
4. What do I want him to know about me?

5. Should I accept future dates with him?

Assume nothing. The courting phase continues until a woman has received a formal request to become a man's girlfriend, and she has said yes!

It is a time for newly introduced strangers to question each other and find out if they are compatible.

The courting phase is positioned at point zero (0) on the MOD relationship continuum because this is an exploratory time, for both the man and woman. During this time of discovery, the woman must be patient and watchful of words and body language

Dates, one, two, three, four, and five is a perfect time for a woman to discuss her relationship boundaries, with her potential partner, and to engage in what I call "purposeful dating!"

When does the Courting Phase end?

The courting phase ends when the dating phase begins. The two phases are separated by the first relationship marker that occurs when a man asks a woman to be his girlfriend.

In essence the courting phase ends when you accept a man's request to be his "official" girlfriend. Becoming a man's girlfriend means that you and he may be viewed as a dating couple. During the courting phase, you are simply acquaintances getting to know each other. It would be wise to engage in purposeful conversations, and strategic dates that will help a woman to decide if her suitor is a player, stringer, creeper, or keeper? It is a time for a woman to control her emotions, stay alert for "red flags" that point to dishonesty or a lack of integrity. It is a time to weed out "Mr. Wrong," before getting emotionally or sexually involved.

Each relationship marker is an important part of the foundation on which the MOD! Close the Deal: Marry Your Guy in 6 Months to 1 Year commitment blueprint is built. Plain and simply stated, it is the man's responsibility to do the asking, and not the woman.

Never again, will a woman have to wonder or ask this question: "Am I your girlfriend?" If you have to ask, then the answer is no you're not! And, as long as you are not his official girlfriend, you must not behave as if you are.

Behaving as if you are when you are not, only puts a woman at an emotional disadvantage, and disrupts the steps to the wedding altar action plan.

You understand the Importance of Sex: Never (on Dates 1, 2, or 3) and Why

What dates 1, 2, and 3 mean to a man: When a man asks you out for a second or third date, what it means is that he's interested in getting to know you better, because he felt a good connection with you on date #1. It doesn't mean that he necessarily wants to be "exclusive" or is thinking of committing to a "serious relationship," with you.

He's just enjoying your company, getting to know you, starting to wonder about you.

So what does that mean for you?

It means that the best thing for you is to do is the very same thing. Use those first few dates to simply get to know if you like this guy and if he's good for YOU.

Taking your time like this is good for several reasons:

- You get to make an informed decision about whether he's worth your time

- You prevent yourself from getting too wrapped up in a man before knowing if he IS worth it

- You protect yourself from getting your heart broken (if you're still checking him out and he breaks it off, you haven't yet determined if he was that great and worth the heart ache, right?)

So, even though guys do weird things, this is one instance where you should follow a guy's lead. Treat those early stages of dating just like a man: Take your time, have fun, and look out for you.

What If He Doesn't Call?

There are three reasons a man might choose not to pursue a relationship after those first few dates:

- He didn't feel the right connection with you

- He's emotionally immature and isn't ready for a relationship

He's a player and isn't capable of forming a relationship with you or anyone else.

One of the most important things for a woman to **NOT** do on the very first few dates, **but especially the first date** is to **NOT have sex with a guy.**

Sex

- Some women think they can hook a man with their great sex, foolishly believing he'll want to be with her because she's the nastiest and freakiest woman he ever met. Then there are the women that say they're just having sex "for fun" and they don't care about the guy, but then secretly get sad when he doesn't call anymore. Whatever type of girl you may be and whatever your reasoning is, having sex with a guy you like is the absolute **WRONG** thing to do. The trick is **DO NOT HAVE SEX**. The less a man gets, the more a man wants. Men only want you when they can't have you.

- You may think, "If two people like each other, then what's the problem?" Through a social media site, I asked men this specific question, "Why do guys convince women to give it up, but then treat her like a stranger when she does?" Well, in so many words it came out like this "Men don't treat a t.h.o.t. (That Ho Over There) like a lady of respect." Only a women that doesn't respect or value herself would have sex with man she barely knows on a first, second or third date.

Until you are aware of the common traits of narcissists, pump the brakes on dating!

1. **Not accountable to anyone**- they will never truly apologize for ANYTHING. They will always put the blame on someone else.

2. **No morals or conscience** - marriage or vows means NOTHING to them. Normal rules of society don't apply to them.

3. **Self-seeking/ ulterior motives always** - every kind act they do or say, they expect to be repaid.

4. **Control freaks**- they always NEED to have the last word.

5. **Very fragile ego!** I said a very harmless joke to the narc about him and his whole body froze and he mumbled some unintelligible retort.

6. **Hold grudges** - they will NOT forget any slight, perceived or real. They will want to get revenge at some point.

7. **Can't be alone,** or not for long, with themselves. Need someone there to admire them.

8. **Hate people but need them at the same time.** Since, they're in love with themselves, they can't summon any true love for anyone else- they are spent!

9. **Lovers of chaos and discord!** If you share an experience you had with a narc, people's reactions are usually wow that sounds like a Lifetime movie or Jerry Springer show or some other crazy a** drama filled freak show.

10. **Shallow**: Appearance really matters - especially with somatic narcs, however, not so much to the cerebral "intellectual" narc.

11. **Projectionist, they are!** Why? Without projecting their faults onto others, it is unclear how narcissists could survive! One way to get confirmation of the activities you suspect a narcissist is doing, behind your back, is to simply take note of what he/she is accusing you of and a majority of the time that is exactly what he/she is guilty of.

12. **Lack of empathy** - the narc I knew could not write even a get well note to our coworker that had been in severe car crash. He said he needed to Google what to write.

13. **Need to feel important**: Triangulation- best believe that a narc will use someone or something to incite feelings of jealousy in you.

14. **Pathological liars**- can't believe a word they say.

15. **Delusional**- they make up their own reality and often think that their life is a movie playing on a big screen that they're watching.

16. **Violent** - not necessarily physical abuse but abusive, nevertheless! The abuse is usually emotionally and mentally.

17. **Special and unique**: They all think that they're special and unique.

18. **Immature**: They cannot be counted on to be the "adult in the room" even as a parent!

19. **Duplicitous**- they will do or say anything to get their needs met.

20. **Deceptively charming**: Idealizing is something they love to do, goes along with their delusional fantasy world. It gets them high as you become entranced with them because it enhances their grandiose vision of themselves. **It's empty flattery and done with a goal in mind- to use you for whatever need they want met.**

21. **Never let go,** whether grudges or you- they won't want to lose you as a source of supply.

22. **Toxic:** prolonged exposure in any type of "manipulation-ship" with a narc, i.e. friend, co-worker, lover, spouse**, can be damaging to your health.** You may wonder why your peace and well-being has evaded you. **Warning,** messing

with these types can cause the following symptoms: high blood pressure, stomach aches, low self-esteem, anxiety, depression, autoimmune disorders, weight loss/ gain, and overall a sense of general un-wellness.

23. **Manipulative**: this is the narc's mode of operation. They manipulate people to get their needs met. Sometimes, a narc may unwittingly admit that they are manipulative! They can sense when another person is too smart to fall for their "love bombing ploy!"

24. **Sexually perverted**, in the sense that they will engage in demeaning sexual acts and you are simply a blow up doll or sex toy in their eyes.

25. **They may emotionless, for the most part**! You broke up first? Well, to the narc, they will make sure to inform everyone that it was actually them who initiated the split- that is, if it isn't beneficial to play the "victim" role.

NEVER PUT YOURSELF INTO "VOLUNTARY RELATIONSHIP LOCKDOWN!"

When you first meet a guy, he tells you many things that you want to hear, and your emotions are being satisfied on every level and from all directions. He's calling you, asking to take you out, and probably spending money on you, too. Just because he's doing these things with your and for you should not cause you to put yourself into "voluntary relationship lock-down!" In fact it would be a mistake to do so.

From the start, you must exercise patience, and allow him the time, and give him the space to show a willingness to **begin** a commitment to you.

The process of him (your guy) "locking you down, begins when he formally asks you to be his girlfriend. IIe is asking you to "go steady" with him.

Sometimes a guy will plan a romantic date, and give you a small diamond ring to celebrate this occasion.

Asking a woman to be his girlfriend is the first step in the "lock-down" process. It also initiate the male's journey of commitment (to you). He is asking you to accompany him out of the "courting" pool of suitors.

This is an important relationship marker, and it moves the two of you from the initial "courting phase to the "Dating" phase. Officially dating each other as boyfriend and girlfriend does not guarantee exclusivity.

What it means to a woman can mean something totally different to a man.

So, before a woman starts planning her wedding and looking up names for their first born, it's best to take a "chill pill" and relax.

Now is the time to engage in purposeful dating with your boyfriend, and to ask questions that can reveal his true intentions and thought of where the relationship is going.

It is a period of discovery for both of you as a dating couple!

Each phone call, and date that you take should include meaningful questions that will help both of you to decide whether or not, spending more time together is what you want, or not..

It is perfectly appropriate for a woman to establish an "expiration" date for exclusivity, with him.

A reasonable time for a woman to be in a holding pattern with one suitor as his girlfriend is 6 months, maximum. At the end of 6 months the boyfriend is expected to "bust a move in one direction or the other, and make his intentions known to her about his future with her. It is only the right thing to do, as not to tie up her time.

If marriage to you is in his future, and he would like to keep you to himself, the next logical step for him to keep you on lock-down is to make it official, and "pop the question!" If your boyfriend does not see marriage with you in his future, and marriage is your goal, this is the time for you to re-enter the courting phase to interact with new suitors.

It is advisable to **not** engage in a sexual relationship with your boyfriend, during this exploratory dating phase, of 6 months, for obvious reasons. Many of the reason will be discussed in another chapter, so I won't process those reason now.

When docs the Courting Phase end?

The courting phase ends when the dating phase begins. The two phases are separated by the first relationship marker, that occurs when a man asks a woman to be his girlfriend.

In essence the courting phase ends when you accept a man's request to be his "official" girlfriend. Becoming a man's girlfriend means that you and he may be viewed as a dating couple. During the courting phase, you are simply acquaintances getting to know each other. It would be wise to engage in purposeful conversations, and strategic dates that will help a woman to decide if her suitor is a player, stringer, creeper, or keeper? It is a time for a woman to control her emotions, stay alert for "red flags" that point to dishonesty or a lack of integrity. It is a time to weed out "Mr. Wrong," before getting emotionally or sexually involved.

When a woman behaves as if she more significant in a man's life than she is, only puts her in an emotional disadvantage, and disrupts the steps to a man becoming committed to her naturally.

A woman of the marrying kind, doesn't "play" hard to get, she is hard to get! Men are hunters, and they fall in love with the challenge of working for (and earning) a woman's hand in marriage.

Therefore, each relationship marker has certain qualifiers that must be met, passed or demonstrated to advance and move forward to the next level of the relationship commitment blueprint.

Therefore, until a man asks a woman to be his girlfriend, then she is not to provide "girlfriend" benefits, or tell others that she is (his girlfriend). A man that's into a woman will meet her standards and respect her boundaries, when she clearly makes them known, to him.

Becoming one man's "official" girlfriend is the relationship marker that initiates the dating phase, and a man's interest in becoming exclusive with her.

There are specific relationship markers that must be earned by "Mr. Right" before YOU grant access in a sexual way (with him). Of course, many women will laugh this off and continue to allow their emotions to dictate the right time to have sex with a man, and let a man tell them when to have sex with him. So tell me this, how has that worked out for you?

Your honesty with a man, and refusal to cross relationship boundaries, without specific markers in place, will make the right inference (to him) about your strength of conviction to stand on your values and high self-esteem.

Believe it or not, men are actually turned on by women that make them work to earn them, step by step, and often times triggers thoughts of him marrying this "high value woman," way before the woman knows it!

Men treat all women in the same way, and that is: the way women allows them too.

Every day, is a day to be awesome, and to represent your brand well!

Your actions and the way that you carry yourself speaks volumes!

When marriage to your special guy is what your goal is, don't settle for gifts, trips, or expensive vacations. Accepting these things rarely leads to anything other than premature intimacy, as a pay back! Reminder: Control your emotions, and keep your emotional shield raised!

It doesn't matter how perfect a woman looks, she will be treated like a common t.h.o.t. (that ho over there) the minute she gives into a guy, without him putting in the EFFORT to prove that she is special to him, and that he is committed to her!

Basically, men pretend they want a woman who "doesn't play games" and is "mature," and can handle sex with no strings, but these are just "player" lines to get a woman to go to bed with them, and to get you committed to them without them proving that they are committed to you

Traits of "High-Value" women of the "marrying kind:

- **Respect yourself.** To men, a respectful woman has boundaries. A woman with no boundaries, allows the man to set her boundaries according to his interests. He treats her in ways that demonstrates that she is there for his pleasure, and not for developing a loving relationship that leads to marriage. The tone in his voice when he speaks to you, the words that he speaks, the lack of use of cuss words in front of you, and his manners should always be on the respectful level with you in his presence.

- **Don't play "Hard to Get: Be hard to get!** Men want to get the girl that's a challenge and doesn't give it up easily. The girl that makes him wait for it, work for it, and chase after it. The (h.t.g.) **hard to get** woman is the woman they really want. This type of woman (the h.t.g. woman) is not playing hard to get games either! She **is** hard to get! A man knows and recognizes that a true queen or diva (of the marrying kind) is the woman that has no problem with rejecting a bullshitter, in his tracts, including but not limited to him!

- **Never act "thirsty"** or act like you want to have sex quickly, because it's an "unqueenly-like, un-lady-like, un-smart indicator that will weaken your brand, and render you "powerless!"

- **Make him put in some effort** to show that you are special and mean the world to him. The type of woman a man will love gives off a vibe that says loud and clear: "I'm not an easy t.h.o.t. - type of woman, and you're going to have to put in some effort, if you want a girl like me, because I'm very special."

- **Create an opportunity for him to demonstrate** his words of affection (that he has expressed to you). Test his loyalty to you, way before you give in to any one of his requests! Giving away your time, companionship, body, is never a wise thing to do, especially when your goal is for your guy to marry you! Trust and believe that the harder he has to work to prove that he is committed to you, the sooner he will pop the question, and marry you!

- **Summary:** If a guy pressures you for sex from early on in the courting phase and you refuse to cooperate, and he leaves you alone, he was just out to freak you and forget you, so aren't you glad you didn't give it up to him?

He was only looking for SEX. ~ Don't try to convince yourself it was anything less than him trying to use you. When you're out in the dating world, this is going to happen... a lot. So, don't take it personally when it happens. You have to take it for what it is: There are lots of players and stringers out there having a good time at the woman's expense.

Stop Dating Until …….. You Are Ready!